A SMALL ★ SURPRISE

Jobs available apply within

Small animals need not apply

Louise Yates

Jonathan Cape
London

I
am
small.

I
am
too

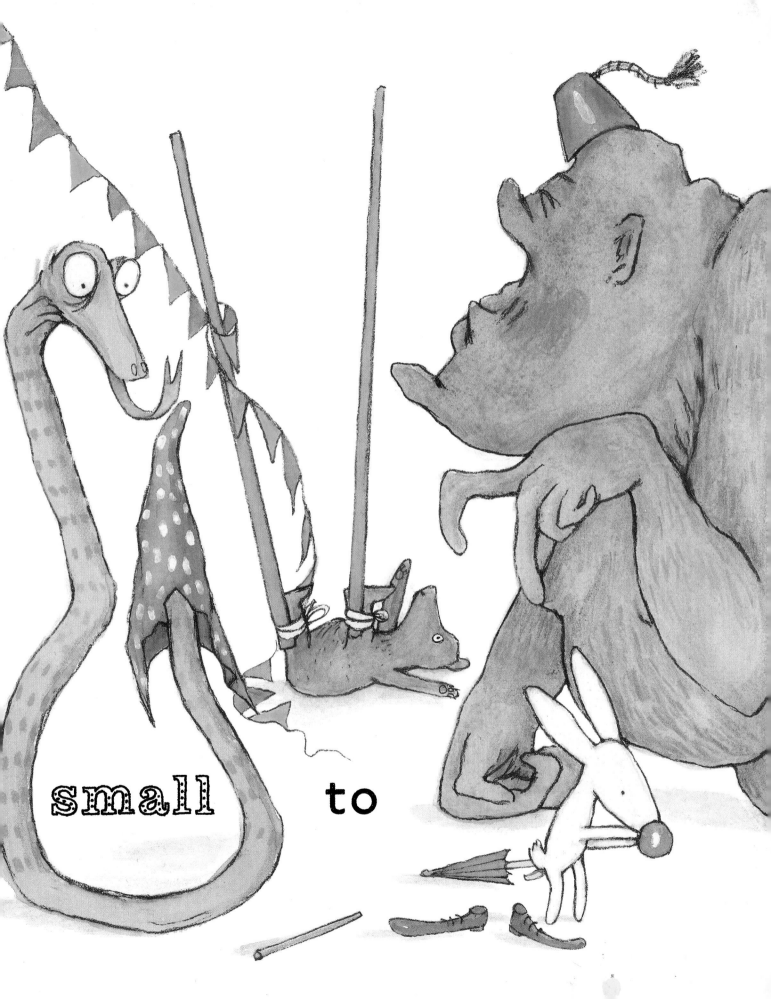

small   to

wipe

my

own

nose.

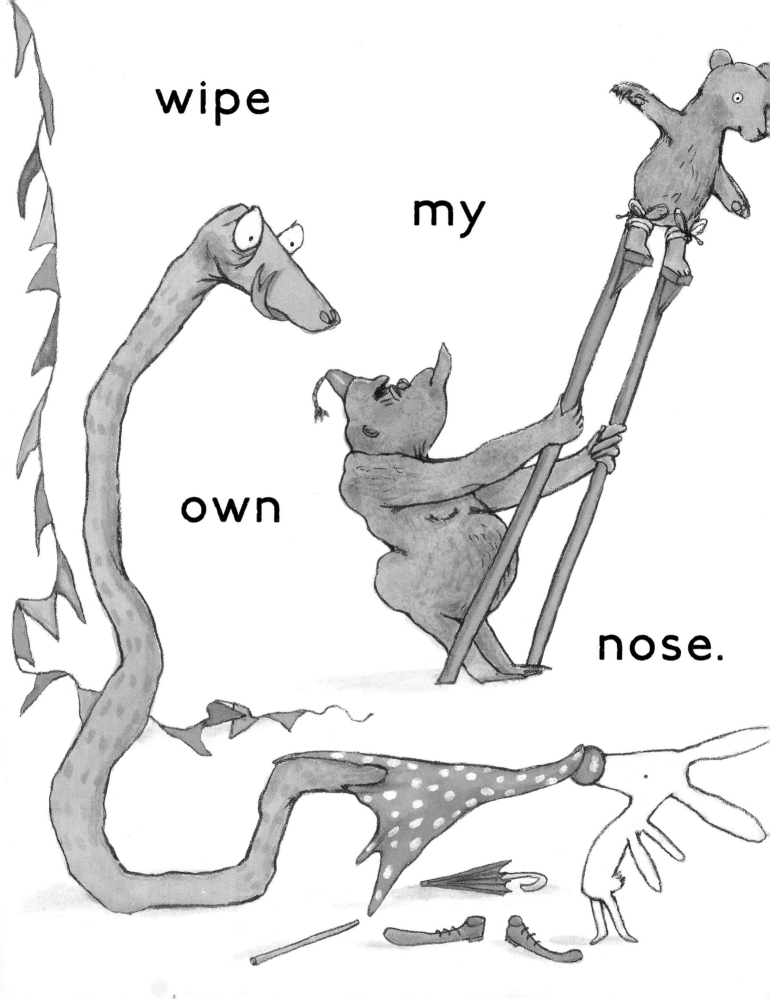

I am

too

small to

tie

my

own

shoes.

I am

too small to walk far

without

needing a

rest,

eat my food

without

making a mess.

But

I
am
just
the right size

to

disappear.

and  repppear.

to

and

to

disappear.

and reappear

and

that's

what

makes

me

For the people who told me
not to dedicate this to them
~ JY, AY and TD ~
a small surprise,
with love
x.

A SMALL SURPRISE
A JONATHAN CAPE BOOK 978 0 224 08341 6

Published in Great Britain by Jonathan Cape, an imprint of Random House Children's Books
A Random House Group Company

This edition published 2009

1 3 5 7 9 10 8 6 4 2

RANDOM HOUSE CHILDREN'S BOOKS 61–63 Uxbridge Road, London W5 5SA

www.kidsatrandomhouse.co.uk www.rbooks.co.uk

Addresses for companies within The Random House Group Limited can be found at: www.randomhouse.co.uk/offices.htm

THE RANDOM HOUSE GROUP Limited Reg. No. 954009
A CIP catalogue record for this book is available from the British Library.

Printed in Malaysia

Magical
MENAGERIE
Shortest
SNAKE
SERIOUSLY SAVAGE
NO
vacan
Smallest
bravest
most interesting